Diamond
the Magic Unicorn

For Alice and Henry xx – SK
For TS – ST

SIMON AND SCHUSTER
First published in Great Britain in 2012 by Simon and Schuster UK Ltd
1st Floor, 222 Gray's Inn Road, London WC1X 8HB
A CBS Company
Text copyright © 2012 Sarah KilBride
Illustrations copyright © 2012 Sophie Tilley
Concept © 2009 Simon and Schuster UK
The right of Sarah KilBride and Sophie Tilley to be identified
as the author and illustrator of this work has been asserted by them
in accordance with the Copyright, Designs and Patents Act, 1988
All rights reserved, including the right of reproduction in whole or in part in any form
A CIP catalogue record for this book is available from the British Library upon request
ISBN: 978-0-85707-441-6
eBook ISBN: 978-0-85707-705-9
Printed in China
3 5 7 9 10 8 6 4 2

Princess Evie's Ponies

Diamond the Magic Unicorn

Sarah KilBride

Illustrated by Sophie Tilley

SIMON AND SCHUSTER

London   New York   Sydney   Toronto   New Delhi

At Starlight Stables Princess Evie had been practising showjumping with her pony, Diamond. "That was so much fun," she smiled. "Why don't we go on an adventure?"

You see, Evie's ponies weren't just any old ponies. They were magic ponies! Whenever Evie rode them, she was whisked away on a magical adventure in a faraway land.

Diamond stamped her hoof excitedly.
She couldn't wait to see where they would go today!

Princess Evie raced back from the tack room
with her rucksack of useful things,
followed by her kitten, Sparkles.

In no time at all, they were
cantering through the tunnel of trees towards
their new adventure. Princess Evie closed her eyes.
Where would the tunnel take them today?

When Princess Evie opened her eyes, they were cantering into a world of shimmering clouds. Diamond now had a golden unicorn's horn and Evie was wearing sparkly riding boots, jodhpurs and a glittering riding jacket.

Trotting towards them on a unicorn was a cloud sprite with
flowers in her hair. "Hello, I'm Skye and this is Jewel," she said.
"We're going to the Unicorn Games, would you like to come?"
"Unicorn Games?" gasped Evie "We'd love to!"
"Brilliant," said Skye.

At the Unicorn Riding Stables, the cloud sprites were busily preparing for the games. Skye and Evie joined them, combing the unicorns' manes and making sure their horns and hooves gleamed. Skye explained that a unicorn's hooves were so magical, they barely left any hoof prints.

Just then, Rosy, the organiser, appeared looking very worried.

"I can't find the medals," she said.

"Don't worry," said Evie. "We'll help you."

They searched in all the buckets, under piles of hay and in
every stable block, but they were nowhere to be found.

"What are we going to do?" cried Rosy. "We can't
have the Unicorn Games without prizes!"
"Don't worry, I think Sparkles has found just the thing," smiled Evie.

Sparkles was playing with a tangle of ribbons
that he'd pulled from Evie's rucksack.
"Fantastic!" said Skye. "We can make rosettes."

In no time at all, the girls had made a pile of beautiful,
bright rosettes. Now the competition could start!

The first event was rainbow jumping. Diamond nuzzled Evie as they waited their turn. They managed to clear the first three jumps but, as the rainbows became higher and higher, Diamond found it more difficult.

The last jump was by far the highest and, even though Diamond
jumped as high as she could, she couldn't clear it.

"Never mind, Diamond," said Evie.
"I'm so proud of you for trying your best."

Diamond and Evie thought the next event sounded really exciting – cloud bursting! When the ring was full of little clouds, the unicorns sped off, popping as many clouds as they could with their horns.

Soon, all the clouds were gone and it was
time to count up who had burst the most.

The winners were Skye and her unicorn, Jewel,
who popped ten clouds! Diamond had managed to pop five.

"It doesn't matter if we don't win," said Evie.

"We're having so much fun."

The final event was the obstacle race. Evie thought
they may be able to win this one.

At the sound of the whistle, all the competitors dashed
into the arena and completed each of the challenges as
quickly as they could.

The crowd cheered, as the unicorns and their riders galloped around the ring! What an exciting finish! It was a tie between Jewel and Diamond!

The judges went to check the course to see which unicorn had completed it without leaving a single hoofprint. Everyone waited anxiously for the result. The winner was . . .

. . . Diamond!

"Congratulations!" said Skye. "You deserved to win."

"We have decided to award Sparkles a special prize,"
said Rosy, placing a rosette on his collar. "Without
him, the games would not have happened!"

At the prize-giving, all the unicorns wore their colourful rosettes. The unicorns neighed and shook their shimmering manes, and their riders cheered.

Sparkles proudly wore his rosette as Diamond took him and Evie on a lap of honour around the ring.

"What an exhausting day!" laughed
Princess Evie. "But great fun."
"Please come next year," said Skye.

Sparkles gave a loud miaow.
"I think that means we'd love to," said Evie.

Evie and Sparkles hopped up onto
Diamond. They said their goodbyes and were
soon galloping towards the tunnel of trees.

When they got back to Starlight Stables, Evie took off Diamond's saddle and brushed her coat and mane. "Thank you so much for today," she whispered.

Just as she was about to go, Evie spotted a
pair of riding gloves on the stable door.
Each one was decorated with a golden unicorn.

"What a lovely present," smiled Evie. "Thank you, cloud sprites.
We'll never forget our unicorn adventure."

"Miaow," agreed Sparkles.

Also available:

Neptune the Magic Sea Pony
Silver the Magic Snow Pony
Willow the Magic Forest Pony
Star the Magic Sand Pony
Shimmer the Magic Ice Pony
Indigo the Magic Rainbow Pony

Coming soon:

Confetti the Magic
Wedding Pony